GIRLS SURVIVE

Girls Survive is published by Stone Arch Books, an imprint of Capstone.
1710 Roe Crest Drive
North Mankato, Minnesota 56003
www.capstonepub.com

Library of Congress Cataloging-in-Publication Data is available on the Library of Congress website.

ISBN: 978-1-4965-9691-8 (hardcover)
ISBN: 978-1-4965-9911-7 (paperback)
ISBN: 978-1-4965-9762-5 (eBook PDF)

Summary: When her mother announces a holiday vacation to Thailand, Tara isn't thrilled. She'd rather stay home with her friends, but Mom is determined they use the girls' trip to explore their Thai heritage. Tara is reluctant to travel so far from home, especially to a country she doesn't feel connected to. But then disaster strikes. The day after Christmas, a massive tsunami hits Thailand. Tara's resort vacation suddenly becomes a fight to survive—and find her mother in the wreckage.

Image Credits
Cover art by Jane Pica

Shutterstock: Spalnic, (paper texture) design element, Studiojumpee, (thai pattern) design element

Designer: Kayla Rossow

TARA
AND THE
TOWERING WAVE

An Indian Ocean Tsunami Survival Story

by Cristina Oxtra

illustrated by Francesca Ficorilli

STONE ARCH BOOKS
a capstone imprint

CHAPTER ONE

Mom and I made our way through the busy
airport in Thailand. I stayed close as we headed
toward the main entrance, dragging our heavy
suitcases behind us. I didn't want to get separated
in the sea of travelers. Many of them were families
rushing to grab suitcases and hurrying off to
wherever they had to be.

There was so much energy and excitement
around me. It seemed like people couldn't wait
for their trips or vacations to start. I wasn't quite
as thrilled about mine.

"Tara, you're right up against me," Mom said. "Be careful. You almost tripped me with your suitcase."

"Sorry, Mom," I said. "I just don't want to get lost in the crowd."

"You'll be fine," assured Mom. "I'm not going to leave you behind."

Despite her assurances, I was nervous. I had only flown in an airplane once before, and that had been to Texas. My dad had received an award from his company, and Mom and I had attended a banquet in San Antonio to celebrate with him.

Flying to Thailand was my first overseas trip. Mom and I had traveled more than twenty hours, flying from Minneapolis, Minnesota, to Phuket, an island off the coast of southern Thailand. We were thousands of miles away from home. This was a whole new world for me.

Honestly, I wasn't sure I wanted to be there. I would have rather been at home, sitting by the fireplace in our townhome, reading a book and sipping hot cocoa. Or snow tubing with my best friend, Abby. Or, better yet, with Mom and Dad, planning the dinner menu for our annual Christmas party at the big house we used to live in.

We'll probably never do that again, I thought. It had been two years since my parents had divorced, and we hadn't heard from Dad since.

A few feet from the main exit doors, we approached a man holding a sign that said *Thai Orchid Resort shuttle.*

"That's our ride," Mom said.

The man welcomed us and led us outside to the resort shuttle van. He loaded our luggage in the back.

"Please take a seat," he said. "We will wait for our other guests, then head to the resort."

"How far away is the resort?" I asked.

"It will take a little more than an hour to drive there," the man replied.

I nodded and boarded the van, grabbing a seat next to the window before anyone else could take it. Mom sat next to me. The sun filtering through the window was warm and comforting, especially after coming from the snowy Minnesota winter.

I never thought I would be spending Christmas in Thailand. When Mom first said she wanted to take a vacation, I thought she'd meant Wisconsin Dells. Maybe Disneyworld. But a few months ago, over dinner at home, Mom had waved a pair of airline tickets in front of me.

"Guess what? With all the extra hours I've worked at my new job, I've saved up enough money for us to go on a girls' getaway!" she announced. "We're going to Thailand!"

I had coughed up the spoonful of macaroni and cheese that I had just inserted into my mouth. "We're going where? You're joking, right?"

She was not.

"This is a once-in-a-lifetime adventure, Tara. We're going to learn more about Thailand and connect with our Thai heritage," Mom said. She reached out and placed a hand on mine. "We're going to take a break and spend time together, where your grandparents came from. It's going to be great. You'll see."

Mom had never been to Thailand. Neither had I. But her parents—Grandma Samorn and Grandpa Panit—were Thai. They were from Khao Lak, a beach town on the west coast of Thailand. They had been young and newly married when they immigrated to America in the mid-1960s.

They had started out in California, then moved to Minnesota to establish a quiet life. Grandpa had worked in construction while Grandma had found work as a seamstress. They had known enough English to get by and had taught themselves more by watching TV and reading.

I had never gotten to know my Thai grandparents. They had passed away in an accident when I was four years old. I didn't remember much about them, other than what Mom had told me.

I wonder what they would've thought about us visiting Thailand, I thought as we set out for the resort.

I watched out the window as scooters and motorcycles—some carrying several people—zipped in and out of traffic. They drove quickly, squeezing in between cars and buses. The traffic on the road was chaotic and felt nothing like home. But somehow everyone seemed to know what they were doing.

The van traveled on, eventually crossing the bridge that linked Phuket Island to Phang-nga. As we edged closer to Khao Lak, the busy traffic gave way to greenery, palm trees, fields, and open spaces. Shops and roadside eateries lined the highway. The signs above them were in Thai and English.

Finally, we arrived at the Thai Orchid Resort. Mom and I made our way to a counter carved with ornate designs and stood in line waiting to check in. Chandeliers shaped like cascading waterfalls above us and bay windows all around provided plenty of light. Several large sofas, cushy chairs, and tables with vases of orchids were spread across the patterned tile floor.

I heard conversations in languages I didn't recognize and was glad to see so many other tourists in the resort. When Mom had first told me about the trip, I'd been worried we would stick out. But that clearly wouldn't be the case.

"There are a lot of tourists here, Mom," I said.

Mom nodded. "December is prime tourist season. A lot of people from Europe and Australia come here to celebrate the holidays in the sun," she said.

When it was our turn to check in, we approached a young woman with a bright smile. Her dark hair was tied neatly in a bun atop her head. Like the other employees, she wore a long, black skirt and a short-sleeved lilac blouse with a gold basket-weave pattern. The colors reminded me of an orchid.

"*Sawatdee kha.* Hello," she greeted us. "Welcome to the Thai Orchid." The woman bowed her head and placed the palms of her hands together in front of her, just under her eyebrows, as though in prayer.

Mom raised her hands up like she was about to do the same gesture in return. Instead, she ended up awkwardly waving both hands. "Hi," she said.

"I am Malee," the woman said, pointing to the gold name tag pinned to her blouse. "I will check you in today. What is the name on the reservation?"

"Jennifer Simon," Mom answered. "That's me."

Malee looked up Mom's name on the computer in front of her. As she typed on the keyboard, she glanced at me and smiled.

"I'm Tara," I told Malee.

"Nice to meet you, Tara," Malee said. "How old are you?"

"Twelve," I replied.

"You are a little beauty," said Malee.

My cheeks felt warm. I must have blushed. "Um . . . thanks."

"Are you Thai?" asked Malee.

"Half," I said. "My grandparents are . . . I mean, were . . . Thai. They used to live somewhere around

here until they moved to America. But they died when I was little."

"I'm sorry to hear that," said Malee. She then looked to Mom. "So just the two of you visiting?"

Mom rubbed the back of her neck, like she did whenever she was stressed. I wondered if she was thinking the same thing I was: *This would have been a nice family vacation if Dad were here.*

"We're on a holiday getaway. Just us girls," Mom said with a forced grin.

"We're from Minnesota, in America," I added. "This is our first time in Thailand."

"Ah, well you've come to the right place," Malee said. "You'll have a wonderful time. If there is anything I can do to help, please let me know."

Malee waved over a young man in black trousers and a short-sleeved, button-down shirt the same color as her blouse. "This is Thanom," she said. "He will take you to your bungalow."

I turned to Mom. "Aren't we staying in a hotel room?"

"I thought it would be more fun to stay close to the pool," Mom explained. "This way we'll be just a short stroll away from the beach."

Thanom placed our suitcases on a luggage cart and began to push it. "This way, please," he said.

"Enjoy your stay." Malee waved at us.

"Thanks. Bye," I said, waving back.

Mom and I followed Thanom outside the main hotel building. He led us to a lush, flower-filled garden that housed several small, one-story buildings with thatched roofs. They looked like private homes, but were actually the resort bungalows.

Our bungalow had wooden floors and a cozy living room with comfortable furniture made of wood and wicker. Everything was decorated with cushions in colorful fabrics.

The two beds in the bedroom were covered in pure white sheets and fluffy pillows. A nightstand stood in between the beds. Everything looked so inviting and luxurious, like we were princesses in our own tropical palace.

When Thanom left, Mom opened the bedroom window. I peered out and inhaled the fresh salt sea air. I had never been so close to the ocean before. I could see the vibrant blue water in the pool, and just beyond that was the turquoise ocean.

It looked peaceful, but nothing like the lakes in Minnesota. When I stood on the lakeshore at home, I could see where the water ended. I could figure out where the land was on the other side. Not with the ocean. It seemed to stretch forever.

As I stared out at the water, I felt so small in comparison. The ocean looked calm now, but I suspected that if it wanted to, the water could swallow me.

CHAPTER **TWO**

Mom and I spent Christmas Day relaxing by the beach. It was strange to spend the holiday in eighty-degree weather, basking in the sun on a tropical island. Sure, snow was great for Christmas in Minnesota. But maybe this wasn't so bad either.

The following day, Mom woke me up early.

"I was thinking we could go to the open-air market this morning before it gets too hot," she suggested. "We can do some shopping, buy some souvenirs. You might find something nice for Abby."

"Yeah, I'm sure she'd like a souvenir," I said.

"We can eat there too," Mom added. "It'll be more fun than having breakfast here at the resort again. Then we can come back, hang by the pool, and figure out what else we want to do."

"Are you sure about eating at the market?" I asked, wrinkling my nose. "What if we get sick?"

"Of course I'm sure," Mom said. "Come on, Tara. We're on an adventure, remember? Don't be afraid to try new things. Keep an open mind. Okay?"

I sighed. "Okay."

I put on my swimsuit and added a pair of jeans shorts and sandals. Then I pulled out the new floral shirt Mom had given me the day before as a Christmas gift and slipped it on.

"That looks nice," Mom said, coming to stand next to me.

I smiled as Mom turned away and slipped her feet into the flip-flops I had given her. I had saved

the money I'd earned doing chores to buy them.
Then we paused in front of the mirror in our room.

"Think of everyone else wearing winter coats back home," I said. "And here we are dressed for summer weather."

"We're lucky," Mom said.

She's right, I thought. I was lucky to be on this trip and spend time with Mom. I had grown closer to her since my parents' divorce. In a way, I had already lost one parent. I didn't want to lose the other.

As I studied our reflections, I wondered how Mom had coped when Grandma and Grandpa had died. She had to have been pretty tough to go through that. Mom and I had friends, but we were on our own as far as family. All we had was each other.

I don't know what I would do if I lost her, I thought.

Mom hooked her arm into mine. "Come on, the market awaits!"

At the front desk in the lobby, Malee was already at work. "Good morning, ladies! How are you today?" she asked.

"Fine. Thanks," I answered. "Mom wants us to go to the market for breakfast and shopping."

"Good idea!" Malee said.

"Do you know how we can get a tuk-tuk to the market?" Mom asked Malee. "I know it's just a few blocks away, but I really want to ride in one."

I had seen a picture of a tuk-tuk in a magazine I had read on the plane to Thailand. It was part-car, part-motorcycle and had three wheels. It was called a tuk-tuk because of the sputtering sound its engine made. It didn't look or sound very safe—especially given the traffic I'd seen when we arrived.

"It's not that far. We can walk," I suggested.

"That won't be necessary. I can help you," Malee said. She turned to one of the men who unloaded luggage from the shuttle vans. "Can you please arrange for a ride for our guests? They'd like to take a tuk-tuk to the market."

The man nodded, and a few minutes later, a blue-and-orange tuk-tuk pulled up to the resort's main entrance. On its roof was a sign with the word *TAXI* in bold letters.

It didn't look like any taxi I had ever seen, but Mom's face lit up. "Come on, Tara! Let's go."

Malee waved at us as we walked out to our ride. "Have fun!" she called. "Goodbye!"

The driver was in front while Mom and I sat in a cushioned seat behind. As the tuk-tuk exited the resort grounds and merged onto the main road, *putt-putt-putting* all the way, I had a moment of panic. The tuk-tuk felt rickety.

What if it's too weak to carry our weight? I worried. *What if it collapses in the middle of the road?*

But as the ride went on, I realized I liked it. It was like riding a motorcycle, but with a roof overhead.

Maybe more like a horse-drawn carriage, except with a motor instead of a horse.

When we arrived at the market, I was surprised to see the area already buzzing with activity. Even though it was early, vendors were already set up.

Every stall had something interesting to offer. There were mountains of fragrant spices and different types of rice, fruits of all colors and sizes, and rows of whole fishes. I was surprised to see them out in the open, not plastic-wrapped, like they were in grocery stores back home.

Customers gathered around food stalls and carts, where fruits, vegetables, noodles, and meats were being sliced, chopped, cooked, and fried. All sorts of foods were displayed on tables, while more sizzled on open grills.

The food at the market was so much more fascinating than what had been served at the resort so far. Maybe it was the simple way everything was

presented—on sticks or banana leaves, instead of fancy plates and shiny silver trays. Or maybe it was the way vendors called out to customers. They waved them over, smiled, and introduced the dishes, trying to convince customers to try a bite.

My stomach grumbled, and my mouth watered. Hunger, along with the tempting sights and smells, erased any worries I'd had about eating at the market.

"I'm starving," I said.

"Then let's dive in!" said Mom. "Where should we start?"

"Over there." I pointed to a packed stall a few feet away. Customers sat around small tables as they dug their spoons into steaming bowls. Judging from the looks on their faces, whatever they were eating was well worth the wait.

Mom nodded. "Sure! Where there's that many people, the food must be good," she said.

"Let's go!" I pulled Mom toward the stall.

We lined up at the stall, which was serving rice porridge with slices of meat and vegetables. I used chopsticks to pick up the meat and a deep plastic spoon to slurp up the porridge. It was the perfect combo of salty and savory, and I ate until I could see the bottom of my bowl.

After we finished at the first stall, Mom and I wandered around. In between buying souvenirs, we snacked our way through the market. I ate as many different foods as I could: grilled chicken, beef, and pork; noodles; sweet, sticky rice with mango; custard-filled bread; and a smoothie sipped through a straw in a plastic bag.

Eventually, Mom glanced at her cell phone. "It's ten-twenty. Should we head back to the resort and go to the pool?"

"Yeah, I'm with you," I said, rubbing my belly. "I can't eat another bite."

"Let's start heading back toward the main road. We can grab a tuk-tuk back," Mom suggested.

We weaved around the crowd and along the path that divided the rows of vendors on both sides. The market had grown even busier since we'd arrived. There were more people wandering around in the maze of aisles.

Mom inched a little ahead of me, and I trailed behind, still amazed by everything around me. I turned to catch a glimpse of a stall selling decorative masks when a low rumbling sound, like a motor, caught my attention. Out of nowhere, a scooter whizzed by.

I yelped and jumped out of the way. The scooter had just narrowly missed hitting me and kept on going. But as I caught my breath, I realized the rumbling hadn't stopped, even though the scooter had sped off. Instead, it grew louder.

It was now a roaring, rumbling sound, almost like a train coming in. But I didn't remember seeing train tracks on our way to the market.

Maybe it's a plane, I thought.

I raised my head to the sky, but there was nothing but clouds. No one else seemed bothered. Everyone continued going about their business. But then, in the distance, I heard screams.

Other people must have heard them too because they finally stopped and looked around. Everyone seemed to be trying to figure out what was going on.

I stepped out of the stall and looked in the direction of the sound—now a combination of frightening screams and shouting. The rumble was still there, under it all.

To my horror, a massive wall of water—larger than any I had ever seen—was barreling toward the market. It was destroying and carrying away everything in its path.

I dropped the shopping bags in my hands and lunged forward, grabbing Mom's hand. "MOM!" I screamed. "RUN!"

CHAPTER THREE

Khao Lak, Takua Pa district
Phang-nga, Thailand
December 26, 2004
10:30 a.m.

WHAM! The full force of the water slammed into us. The impact was so strong it knocked the wind out of me.

In the blink of an eye, everyone and everything in the market was washed away. The powerful currents knocked my feet out from under me. Even if I had been able to stand, there was no solid ground on which to set my feet.

In seconds, the street I had been standing on was gone, turned into a churning river. There was nothing but water around me. I tried to hold on to Mom's hand, but I lost my grip.

When I opened my mouth to yell for her, I was sucked under. I quickly clamped my eyes closed, but salty water filled my nose and mouth. I was tossed and tumbled around in the water like a pile of clothes in a washing machine. I couldn't tell which direction was up.

I reached out again, hoping to feel Mom's hand, but there was nothing there. She was gone.

I was mixed in with all sorts of debris. There must have been other people in the water with me too. The market had been packed with tourists and vendors when the wave hit. But it was impossible to tell what anything was in the cold, murky water.

Out of nowhere, something hard smashed into my left arm. If I hadn't been underwater, I would have gasped in pain. I was getting hit on all sides and running out of air. I had to find the surface.

I forced myself to open my eyes underwater, ignoring the sting of salt—and whatever else was also in the water. I had to find Mom. I couldn't see her, but I noticed a glimmer of light somewhere above me.

The surface! I thought, desperate to reach it.

I flailed my arms and kicked, hoping to swim upward. But something tangled itself around my right ankle and calf, holding me captive underwater.

I grabbed at the long, slimy rope. The water made it too murky to see, but it felt like a clump of vines and roots. I wriggled my ankle free and pushed myself up, up, up in the water as fast as I could before I could no longer hold my breath.

When I broke through the top of the water, I gasped for air. More water from the waves around me splashed in, but the rush of oxygen into my lungs made me cough. I heaved up the salty water that I had swallowed.

I treaded water to stay afloat and whirled around and around, hoping to see Mom. The water surged all around me, and I fought to keep my head above the surface.

It was like I had been stranded in the middle of an ocean. All I could see around me was water littered with logs, part of a tin roof, and tree limbs.

There was no sign of Mom. There was no sign of anyone. I couldn't even tell that there had once been a market. I had no idea where I was.

I called out again and again, shouting until my voice was hoarse. "Mom! Mom! Where are you? Can you hear me? Mom!"

No answer. The only sound was the menacing growl of rushing water threatening to carry me away.

A severed tree trunk drifted toward me, and I grabbed on to it. At least now I would have something to hold on to . . . something to help keep my head above water.

I drifted along, clinging to my makeshift floatation device, for a few minutes. All the while

I strained to catch a glimpse of Mom somewhere around me. But just when I thought the worst was over, the roaring, rumbling sound returned. It grew louder and louder.

I reeled around and saw my worst nightmare—another massive wave heading straight for me. The tree trunk was not going to help me stay above water any longer.

I have to find something sturdier to hold on to. Something that won't be swept away by the water, I thought. *If I don't, I'll get pulled under.*

I didn't know if I had the strength to fight my way to the surface again if that happened.

My arm throbbed from being pummeled by debris in the water. Still, I knew I had to move.

Looking around quickly, I spotted a power pole, its upper half still sticking out of the water. I let go of the tree trunk and swam as fast as I could in that direction. I had to make it before the next wave hit.

As soon as I reached it, I wrapped my arms and legs around the thick pole and buried my face into the solid surface. Then I shut my eyes, held my breath, and braced myself.

Just hold on, I thought. *Don't let go. And pray this pole will hold up against the next wave.*

WHAM! Another wave smashed into me. It felt almost stronger that the first. Like the ocean was angry it hadn't washed me away on its first attempt. Instead it had returned, bent on finishing the job.

The waters gushed over and around me. It wasn't like a shower, a rainfall, or a waterfall. This was a thick curtain, determined to suffocate and bury me.

I wanted to scream, but I bit down on my lower lip to keep my mouth shut. I couldn't afford to swallow any more water. All I could think was, *Please make it stop.*

After what was the longest minute of my life, the wave passed, leaving me chest-deep in water.

My heart thumped violently, like it was about to explode from my body.

I clung to the pole for what seemed like an eternity and tried to ease my erratic breathing. I felt battered and bruised. My shoulders were tight and tense. My arms and legs ached and burned. But still, I gripped the pole tightly. I was afraid to let go in case more waves hit.

I shouted out again over and over. "Mom! Mom! Are you out there?" There was no reply. "Mom! Mom? Is there anyone else out there? Anyone?"

No one answered. It was as if it was the end of the world. I was all alone.

I trembled. The water was freezing. I didn't want to let go of the pole, or leave this sturdy spot, but my grip was starting to slip.

I had to find a way to get out of the water. I was surrounded by fallen trees, pieces of wood, and sheets of metal—probably what was left of homes and shops. Two cars floated past.

I craned my neck further and spotted a dirty, torn-up mattress floating toward me.

That's it, I thought.

I took a deep breath and forced myself to let go of the pole. I was terrified of being untethered, but I knew I had to try.

Instantly, the swirling water pulled at me, trying to sweep me away with the other debris. It took all my strength to make my way to the mattress. After two attempts, I managed to pull myself up on to the damp, squishy surface.

The raging water was moving fast. Moving to the mattress had seemed like a good idea, but I couldn't stay there. I didn't know where it would take me or whether it would be safe. I had to find dry land.

As I tried to figure out a plan, I heard shouting, but I couldn't make out the words. I spun around and saw a man watching me from the balcony of a mostly submerged building. It was to my right, just a short distance ahead. A small child stood next to him. The man was shouting to me in Thai, I realized.

"Help!" I yelled back in English. "Please help!" I waved my arms frantically, hoping he understood.

"Come to us!" the man hollered—in English this time. "We will help you!"

This was my chance. But the current was moving fast. The mattress was about to drift past the building. I had to act fast. If I didn't, I would be swept away.

CHAPTER FOUR

Thai Orchid Resort
Khao Lak, Takua Pa district
Phang-nga, Thailand
December 26, 2004
11:00 a.m.

With every ounce of energy I had left, I used my arms like oars to paddle hard against the raging currents. The water pushed back, trying to sweep me away with it, but I was determined. I had to reach that building.

The man encouraged me. "Keep going!" he shouted. "You can do it!"

The bright, sunshine-yellow building shone like a beacon. Onward I paddled. I was so focused on making it to the building that I didn't see the debris coming toward me.

"Watch out!" the man yelled as a jagged piece of tin roof rushed past. It missed the mattress by inches.

Before I had time to react, a floating ice chest rammed the side of the mattress, almost throwing me off-balance. The impact threatened to push me off course.

"No!" I yelled. I paddled to get out of its way.

"You're okay!" the man called out. "You're almost there!"

I wanted that to be true. I had to keep going. I dug my arms deeper into the water and started humming "Row Your Boat." It was the one thing I could think of to help me maintain the rhythm of my paddling and distract me from how dangerous my task was.

Just when I thought I couldn't possibly paddle any more, I finally reached the side of the building. I stretched out both arms, and the man grabbed them. He hoisted me off the mattress, over the balcony railing, and onto the floor of the building.

As soon as my bare feet touched the floor, my legs buckled. The man caught me and gently eased me down. I watched the mattress rocket past. In seconds, the water had swallowed it up.

"Are you all right?" the man asked. "Are you hurt?"

I examined my arms and legs. They were covered in raw cuts and bruises. I was no longer wearing my sandals.

They must have come off in the water, I realized.

"I don't think anything is broken," I said. "Thank you for helping me."

"You're welcome," he said.

I looked around. "Is there anyone else here? I need to find my mom. We were in the market when—"

My voice broke as I was overcome with emotion. I took a deep breath. I had to stay calm if I wanted to find Mom.

"She has long, black hair and brown eyes, like me," I continued. "She was wearing a purple tunic and black leggings. Maybe you've seen her?"

"I'm sorry. I have not," the man said. "We're the only ones here."

I shook my head in disbelief. "This can't be happening," I said. "Is there any way we can look for her? We have to find help. Maybe we can use something else as a raft, like I did with the mattress? There must be a way. Can you help me? I have to find her!"

The man shook his head. "I would like to help you. But unless we had a boat good enough to make it through that water, we can't go," he said.

"You don't understand. My mom is the only family I have in this world!" I cried. "I can't just stay here doing nothing!"

"Believe me. I understand. I don't want to be here either, but we have to stay put for now," the man explained.

"This is a waste of time! It's crazy to just stand around here!" I insisted.

"It would be crazier for us to go out there," he said pointing at the water. "It's not safe to go anywhere until the water is calmer and no more waves come in."

Looking at the water, I knew he was right. For now, I had no choice but to stay put. It was up to me to find Mom. I couldn't do that if I drowned. Frustrated and exhausted, I sank back onto the floor.

"Don't worry. We will get out of here," the man said. "What's your name?"

I didn't answer. I was in no mood for a conversation that didn't involve finding Mom.

"I'm Kiet," the man introduced himself. "But my family calls me Yuk since I'm tall. It means 'giant.'"

I looked up at him and noticed he was, indeed, tall. Still, I crossed my arms. I didn't care about his name or height. Not unless they had something to do with a plan to get out of there and locate Mom.

"You know, I have to think about someone else's safety too," Yuk said.

He motioned to the little girl hiding behind his leg. She twisted the end of her tank top with her finger and tugged at the ruffled trim on her shorts.

"This is my daughter, Sumana. She's six. We call her Noo because she's usually shy and quiet, like a mouse. That is what *noo* means."

I looked at Noo. Her soft brown eyes and the way she held on to her father reminded me of myself when I was little. I used to hide behind Dad whenever he was talking to someone I didn't know.

"Hi," I said to Noo. She stared back, not saying a word.

Yuk had said Noo was usually shy and quiet, but I thought it was more likely that she was traumatized after what she had just witnessed—everything in front of her demolished and washed away. Then I'd shown up out of nowhere and started shouting at her father about how we should leave the safety of the building.

I leaned down to Noo and said, "I'm sorry. I don't mean to scare you. I'm Tara."

Noo didn't react.

"It's okay. I'm scared too," I added.

"You sound American," Yuk said.

I nodded. "I am. Well, we are. Mom and I.
We're on vacation at the Thai Orchid Resort."

Yuk's face lit up. "Maybe you've met my wife.
She works there. Her name is Malee."

"I know her!" I exclaimed. "She works at the
front desk. She's really nice."

"I'm a manager there. I had the day off, so Noo
and I were doing errands," he explained. "We have
not seen Malee since she went to work this morning."

"She was there when we left," I told him. "She
helped Mom and me get a tuk-tuk to the market."

But looking at the destruction around me, I
realized that didn't mean much. I didn't even know if
the resort was still standing. Now I understood why
Yuk didn't want to be stuck there either. Just as
I wanted to find Mom, he wanted to find Malee.

Yuk bowed his head and went quiet.

I had to break the silence. "Where are we?" I asked, looking around. "Is this a restaurant?"

There were wooden chairs and tables all around us. Napkin dispensers, along with cups and utensils, had been set out. In one corner, a long wooden bar was surrounded by tall bar stools. Behind it were shelves with bottles of varying shapes and sizes.

"It is," Yuk answered. "The water carried you about half a kilometer away from the market."

"How far is that in miles?" I asked.

"About a third of a mile," he replied. "Noo and I were around the corner when the water rushed in. I picked her up and ran here. The door was closed, but I broke through. I scrambled up the stairs to the top floor as the water rose." Yuk paused. "I hope Malee had time to . . ."

I didn't know what to say. I had no idea if Malee was okay. I had no idea if Mom was okay. So instead, I said what I hoped was true: "You helped me. I'm sure someone is helping Malee and my mom right now . . . making sure they stay safe."

Yuk nodded, but he was frowning. I didn't think he believed what I said. I wasn't sure I believed it myself, but I tried to shake away any doubts in my mind.

Mom is okay, I told myself. *She has to be.* In the meantime, I had to stay strong. I had to find a way to get to her.

"Do you have a cell phone?" I asked. "Maybe we can call for help."

"Phones aren't working. The cell towers must have been knocked out," Yuk said. He took his flip phone from the front pocket of his jeans and opened the cover. "See?"

"Is there anything we can use here?" I looked around but couldn't see anything useful for a water escape. "We're at a restaurant, right? At least, we have food and water."

Yuk shook his head. "This floor is only for seating," he replied. "The kitchen is below us—underwater."

"What happened?" I pointed to the water. "How could the ocean reach this far?"

"It was a tsunami," Yuk said. "I heard about one in Japan and Indonesia a few years ago. Many people died there. But I have never heard of a tsunami in Thailand."

I knew about tsunamis from science class in school, but I never in a million years thought I would experience one. They weren't something we worried about in Minnesota. I remembered reading that a tsunami happened after an earthquake. But I hadn't felt anything before the massive waves.

Maybe it happened farther away, I thought. *Maybe it was so far that we didn't feel it or know about it.* I wondered whether that was even possible.

"Why didn't my mom and I hear any sirens? Did we miss the warning?" I asked.

Yuk tilted his head and scrunched his eyebrows. "Warning? What do you mean?"

"Like for a tornado. Where we live, if there's a tornado coming, a siren goes off so we have time to find shelter," I explained. "Even our school does tornado drills to make sure everyone knows how to stay safe in case of a tornado."

Yuk shook his head. "We don't have anything like that," he said.

That was not reassuring.

"Does that mean there could be more waves and we wouldn't know they were coming?" I asked.

Yuk nodded.

"But it's over, right? We're safe here, aren't we?"

Yuk looked at Noo, then back at me. "I don't know if it's over," he said. "But I think we're safe here for now."

"For now" wasn't reassuring.

"What are we going to do if more waves come?" I asked.

"We are on the top floor of a four-story building. The water has already risen above the first three floors," Yuk said. "The only way to go higher is if we climb to the roof."

Considering how fast the water had come in before, I didn't know if we would have enough time to make it to the roof. I hoped we were high enough that another wave couldn't reach us. If a wave—one even larger than the previous two—crashed in, we were doomed.

CHAPTER FIVE

Khao Lak, Takua Pa district
Phang-nga, Thailand
December 26, 2004
12:00 p.m.

I wished I had a watch, so I could tell what time it was. There was nothing for us to do but wait for help to arrive.

This must be what it's like to be marooned on a deserted island, I thought.

Noo was sprawled on the floor, quietly stacking the plastic cups she had gathered to create towers. She built a fence around them using the utensils.

I sat in a chair across from Yuk and drummed my fingers on the table. I grew more worried about Mom with each minute that ticked by without her.

I was trying to think of how I could find her when Yuk broke the silence.

"Tara, tell me about America," he said.

"What?"

"What's it like where you are from?" he asked.

I knew Yuk was attempting to take my mind off my worries. Mom was always finding ways to distract me when I was worried about something.

It must be a parent thing, I thought.

Even though I recognized the tactic, I appreciated it. I told Yuk about the snow in Minnesota, the lakes, my best friend, Abby, and my school. He asked me where my dad was, and I told him about my parents' divorce.

"We haven't heard from him in a long time," I said. "What about you? Tell me about your family."

"I was born in a village farther inland," Yuk said. "My parents and siblings are still there. My father and brothers are farmers, but I didn't want that.

When I was old enough, I moved to Khao Lak to find a job. I started out at the front desk at the Thai Orchid. Eventually I worked my way up to manager."

"Is that how you met Malee?" I asked.

Yuk's eyes sparkled, and he nodded. "I fell in love the minute I saw her," he said. "When Noo was born, it was the happiest day of our lives."

"What will you do if the resort is . . . gone?" I asked.

I didn't want to think about that possibility. But given the destruction around us, miles from the beach, I didn't know how anything close to it could still be standing.

Yuk looked somber. "Malee and I want to save up enough money to start our own business—maybe a restaurant. Malee is the best cook. We want to be able to send Noo to a good school."

"Maybe you can come to America and open a Thai restaurant where we live," I said. "There's no other Thai people where we are. Not that we know of, anyway."

Yuk chuckled. "Oh, I don't think we can do that," he said. "Besides, we're happy here."

"My grandparents did it," I said. "Immigrated to America, I mean. They didn't open a restaurant. But they did well for themselves."

I shared with him stories that Mom told me about my grandparents. How tough and hardworking they had been. How they had made a good life in America so Mom and I could have a good life.

"Mom always tells me that when she was growing up, Grandma and Grandpa told her to learn English, get good grades, and go to college," I said. "They only spoke to her in English, so she only knows a few Thai words that she overheard from them."

"Do you know any Thai?" Yuk asked.

"I only know some basic words, like *hello* and *thank you*," I admitted. "But I can't put a sentence together. Maybe one day I can learn more."

Eventually our conversation ended, and Noo fell asleep on her father's lap. I made my way to the balcony. Like a human lighthouse, I kept watch.

Maybe I can spot Mom from here, I thought, even though I knew it was a long shot. *Maybe she'll find her way to me and I can signal to her.*

But Mom was nowhere to be seen. All around me was a watery, muddy mess. Everything that had been there before had been wiped out, obliterated by the furious waters.

The air was eerily still. The sky was clear and blue with a few puffs of white clouds, just as it had been earlier. Above, it still looked like a picture-perfect postcard from paradise. But the devastation below told a more frightening story.

My throat was scratchy and parched. *All this water around us and nothing to drink,* I thought.

I was about to turn away when I heard voices in the distance.

"Yuk! Someone's coming!" I shouted.

Yuk ran to join me, followed by Noo. We watched as two men rowed a small boat toward us. They edged right up to the building and began speaking to Yuk in Thai.

"What's going on?" I asked, tugging at the end of Yuk's shirt. "What are they saying?"

"They're local fishermen," Yuk explained. "They're offering to take us to a safer place. Somewhere dry, where other people have gathered."

"We have to go," I said. "We can't stay here. And my mom and Malee might be there."

Yuk nodded and turned back to the men, speaking to them again in Thai. Then he lowered Noo into the boat. I climbed in next, followed by Yuk. Noo immediately scrambled closer and perched on her father's lap.

The men paddled along, carefully navigating the gauntlet of debris. Everywhere I turned it looked like bulldozers had come through, trampling, flattening, and crushing everything in their path.

Trees had been uprooted. Buildings, businesses, and homes had been reduced to a tangled mess of wood, metal, and bricks. It was as if a giant had picked them up, turned them upside down, and shaken out their contents.

It was terrifying to think that the ocean could suddenly become so vicious. In a blink of an eye, it had turned into a rampaging monster.

I noticed the soles of a pair of shoes sticking out from beneath a pile of rubble. Was someone still wearing them? I was afraid to find out, so I turned away. I felt sick to my stomach and had to swallow hard to keep from throwing up.

On the other side of the boat, Noo gasped.
I didn't ask why. I didn't want to know what she
had seen.

"Shhh . . . ," I heard Yuk hush her.

When the boat finally reached drier land, we
climbed out and trudged through thick sludge. It
came halfway up my calf, and Yuk had to carry Noo.

We passed mounds of debris the water had
carried along with it as it tore through the town.
Dead fish, an overturned cart, a motorcycle with

only one wheel, a chair with no legs, the remains of
buildings.

My chest tightened when I saw a doll lying
half-submerged in mud. *Where is the child who
owns it?* I thought.

Eventually, we reached a building with a large
storefront window. A sign above it read *Sonny's
Souvenirs.* A man, who I assumed was the store
owner, ushered us in. Yuk set Noo down, and she
immediately grabbed her father's hand.

Inside, among the racks of clothes, scarves, jewelry, and trinkets, about a dozen people, Thai and foreign, had sought refuge. They sat on the muddied floor, huddled together in small groups, and spoke to one another in low voices. Based on the tone, they sounded to be words of comfort.

I slowly walked around the store, scanning the faces of everyone there. I peeked over the shoulders of people who were tending to others—men, women, and children with injuries lying on the ground or cradled in someone's arms.

I made my way around the shop twice, checking every aisle, nook, and cranny, just to be sure. But the more I looked, the more my heart sank. Mom was not there.

CHAPTER **SIX**

Khao Lak, Takua Pa district
Phang-nga, Thailand
December 26, 2004

Yuk was speaking to the store owner when
I interrupted.

"Have you seen my mom?" I asked the man.
"Her name is Jennifer. She's Thai, but American.
She has black hair, brown eyes, and she's wearing
a purple tunic and black leggings."

The man looked at me. His eyebrows were
furrowed and his lips were down-turned. He
shook his head. "No. I am sorry," he said.

Before I could say anything else, the two
fishermen who had brought us to the shop came

over and addressed the store owner. They all nodded like they had agreed on something, then turned to walk out.

"Where are they going?" I asked Yuk.

"To search for more people," he replied.

"Wait! Stop! I want to go with you!" I called to them.

Yuk called to the men, and they stopped and turned around.

"Tara, it's not safe," Yuk said. "You can't go."

I tried to reason with him. "I *have* to go. My mom is out there somewhere. She might be alone and hurt. I have to look for her."

"Wouldn't your mom want you safe and away from the water?"

I raised my voice. "Yuk, I can't just wait here and do nothing. I already wasted too much time waiting at that restaurant. I can't lose my mom! I have to find her!"

Yuk placed his hands on my shoulders and spoke in a low voice. "Okay. Go with them. Find her. I'll stay with Noo and help others here until we can figure out what to do next. Be careful."

"I will."

Yuk and the two fishermen spoke in Thai, then he turned to me. "They will let you go with them. They will take you to the market."

I breathed a sigh of relief. "Thank you," I said. "I'll be back—hopefully with my mom."

I followed the fishermen back outside. After slogging through the muck, we hopped into the boat. We navigated through the water-logged labyrinth— what remained of the town—until we passed the building where Yuk, Noo, and I had been earlier.

A few minutes later, one of the men pointed in front of us and turned to me. "Market," he said.

I looked around, not saying a word. I could not believe this was the same busy market Mom and I had been at earlier. Everything had been washed away in the waves.

Where are the stalls, the tuk-tuks, the food, the people? I thought. *Where did they all go?*

There was no time to think about it. I started yelling, "Mom! Mom! Are you out there?"

Silence.

"Mom! It's me, Tara! I brought help!"

The boat continued to glide along, moving through the brown water. The fishermen looked to the right, to the front, then to left, like searchlights trying to cover as much ground—or water—as possible. Making sure not to miss anyone who might be out there.

Thump! One of the oars hit something.

"What is it?" I asked.

The man didn't answer. He set his oar in the boat and peered over the side to see what it was. The other fisherman and I craned our necks to see too.

I gulped. *Please don't let it be what I think it is.*

The fisherman reached a hand down to the water and pulled out a log. I exhaled loudly.

The man moved the log out of the way and grabbed his oar. Both men resumed paddling, but before we'd gone far, I heard something. It sounded like shouting.

"Wait! Stop! Listen!" I tapped one of the men on his shoulder.

He stopped rowing and turned to me.

"Listen," I said, cupping a hand to my ear. "Do you hear that? It's a voice." I couldn't understand what it was saying.

The man tilted his head as the sound grew louder. Then he motioned to the other man, and they began to row faster.

My pulse raced. *Could it be Mom?*

As we drew closer, I saw a young boy with dark hair and bronze skin. He was dressed in shorts but missing his shirt. With him was an elderly woman in a blue dress. They hollered and waved at us from the top branches of a tree. The water had almost reached the top.

The boy looked to be about my age. He was balanced on a branch a few inches above the gray-haired woman. They were both soaking wet and had gashes on their arms and legs. The boy also had a deep cut across his forehead.

They must have fought to stay above the water like I did, I thought.

The fishermen steered the boat right up to the tree and spoke to the boy, giving him instructions. Then, like an agile cat, the boy leaped off the branch and jumped into the boat, landing on his bare feet.

I thought he might lose his balance and fall out of the boat, so I put my arms out to catch him, but he was steady. The boy turned to the woman and gestured for her to join us in the boat.

"*Ya!*" he called.

The word was vaguely familiar. I remembered my mom telling me to call my grandmother that when I was little. The woman must be the boy's grandmother.

The boy reached out for his grandmother as she slowly, inch by inch, climbed down the tree. The boy talked to her the whole time, giving her what sounded like encouragement. As she reached us, one of the fishermen grabbed her arm while the other steadied the boat. I opened my arms, ready to catch her in case she stumbled as she stepped into the boat, but she made it in.

I scooted to the back of the boat to make room for our new passengers. The boy guided his grandmother to a seat, then sat next to her. She took his hand in hers, and he spoke to her quietly.

I imagined he was saying, "It's all right now, Grandma. We'll get out of here soon." I wanted to say the same to her but didn't know how. I wished Yuk were here to translate.

The men spoke to the newcomers in Thai, then pointed in the direction of the shop. One of the men turned to me and said, "Sonny's."

"Yeah." I nodded. We were headed back to the shop. "Okay."

The grandmother needed to be somewhere safe. I knew that. She was lucky to have made it up the tree. If another wave came along, I was sure she would be swept away. If she had been my grandmother, I would have wanted her safely away from the water too.

But I wasn't okay. We still hadn't found Mom, and I didn't want to go back to the shop without her. Somehow, I had to keep looking.

CHAPTER **SEVEN**

Khao Lak, Takua Pa district
Phang-nga, Thailand
December 26, 2004
2:50 p.m.

I returned with the group to Sonny's Souvenirs. On the one hand, I was relieved we had found the boy and his grandmother. But I would have been much happier if we had found Mom too.

Yuk ran up to me with Noo close behind. "Tara? What happened? Did you find her?"

I shook my head. "No. No sign of her. But we found a boy and his grandmother." I pointed to the pair being welcomed by the shop owner.

"I'm sorry," Yuk said, leaning down to pat my shoulder. "But don't give up hope. We will find her."

I nodded. "If we're going to stay here for the night, I want to go back out there. I need to keep searching."

Yuk shook his head. "We're not staying. There are rumors of more waves possibly reaching farther inland," he said. "I don't know if it's true or not."

The thought of more water coming was terrifying. *Will it ever stop?* I worried.

"Then we have to keep going," I said firmly. "We can't take any chances."

Yuk nodded. "I agree. There are several people going to the hospital. It's about thirty minutes from here," he said. "I will look for Malee there. Your mother might be there too. And a doctor can treat your injuries."

After some talk among the adults, Yuk, Noo, and I piled into the cramped bed of an old pickup truck along with several others, including the boy and his grandmother, and set off for the hospital.

When we arrived, people had already gathered outside in the parking lot and on the grassy grounds.

Noo and I followed Yuk as he entered the big, white building. It was chaos inside the crowded hospital. The cries of people looking for loved ones mixed with the moans of pain from the injured. Everyone wore matching expressions of shock, sadness, and confusion. The smell of sweat and blood filled the air, and splotches of dirt and mud were splattered across the once-white floor.

Yuk approached a desk and spoke to a frazzled woman in a nurse's uniform. She was shuffling a mess of papers, trying unsuccessfully to organize it. She stopped to talk to Yuk. In the blur of Thai conversation, I heard Malee's name.

The nurse riffled through stacks of papers, then typed on the keyboard of the computer in front of her. A moment later, she shook her head.

Yuk sighed deeply. The nurse wrote down his information. Then Yuk said something else in Thai and pointed at me.

The nurse turned to me and spoke in English. "You are looking for your mother?"

"Yes," I said quickly. I told her Mom's name and gave a description. "We were in the market this morning when the wave hit. Have you seen her?"

The nurse checked the papers and her computer again. "I'm sorry. No. What is your name?"

"Tara," I answered. "Well, actually, Chantara. My full name is Chantara Simon. Tara is my nickname."

"Chantara," the nurse repeated. "Pretty name. Are you Thai?"

I paused. "I . . . Yes. I am. But I live in America."

The nurse nodded. "If your mother shows up, I will tell her where you are. For now, you three can rest over there." She pointed to two foldable cots in a crowded area across the hall.

Yuk, Noo, and I made our way over to the empty cots. The ward was filled with patients, both Thai and foreign. Some of the patients' clothes were ripped and dirty. Others were in their swimsuits and bare feet, like they had been plucked straight off the beach and plunked down in the hospital.

After a while, a doctor came over to our cots to examine my cuts and bruises. When he was finished, a nurse gave me a wet cloth to wipe off the mud and dirt. Then she cleaned my cuts and slathered some ointment on them. That was all they could do. They had to hurry to care for the more seriously injured patients who were arriving every few minutes.

Yuk turned to me. "Tara, can you please watch Noo for me? I heard a group of people talking out there. They have a vehicle and will look for more people. I need to get to the resort. I can try to find Malee with their help."

"Yeah. Of course," I replied. I wanted to ask if I could go too, to look for Mom, but watching Noo was the least I could do for Yuk.

Besides, what if Mom comes to the hospital looking for me? I thought. *I should stay here.*

"Keep a lookout for my mom too," I pleaded.

"Yes. I will," Yuk said. "Of course."

He turned and spoke to Noo in Thai. She shot me a nervous look but nodded. Yuk hugged her and kissed her on the forehead.

"I will be back," Yuk said to us.

While Yuk was away, I tried to entertain Noo with games—I Spy, Rock-Paper-Scissors, anything to keep her occupied. I told her stories I remembered my parents telling me at bedtime when I was her age.

I wasn't sure if Noo even understood me. She didn't say anything. But she sat in my lap, leaned back against me, and seemed to be listening, so I kept talking.

When I noticed Noo rubbing her stomach, I figured she was hungry. I glanced at a clock on the wall. 5:45 p.m. Hours had passed since Yuk had left.

"I'm hungry too. And really thirsty," I admitted. "Let's go see what we can find."

I took Noo's hand and returned to the front desk. The same nurse was still there, looking even more frazzled than she had earlier.

"Excuse me," I said. "Is there any water or food?"

The nurse shook her head. "I'm sorry," she said. "The hospital kitchen is closed. We have no one working there. And even if we did, no one knows when supplies will get here. That includes food, water, and medicine."

I thought about the food I'd eaten at the market. *Was that really just this morning?* I thought. I would have done anything to have all that food on hand now.

I had to do something to keep my mind off how hungry and worried I was. With Noo in tow,

I checked other floors and rooms. We ventured outside, where people had started to camp out. I was hoping against hope that I would find Mom.

Maybe the nurse made a mistake, I thought. *Maybe Mom is here somewhere. With so many people coming and going, she could have slipped by.*

I hoped that was true. But none of the faces I saw belonged to Mom.

It was dark when I decided to take Noo back inside. We were both exhausted. We huddled together on my small, uncomfortable cot. Noo rubbed her shoulders.

"Are you cold?" I pretended to shiver. "Brrrrr!"

Noo nodded.

There were no blankets. Since I had my swimsuit under my top, I took off my shirt and put it on Noo. I buttoned it up for her, thinking back to when Mom had given it to me on Christmas morning. That felt like a lifetime ago.

A part of me didn't want to take off the shirt. It was the only piece of Mom I had with me. But Noo needed warmth. She was so little. She needed the shirt more than I did.

Noo snuggled close to me. I closed my eyes and listened to her softly breathing. It was soothing, almost like the sound of the ocean Mom and I had sat by on Christmas Day. Before I knew it, it grew further and further away.

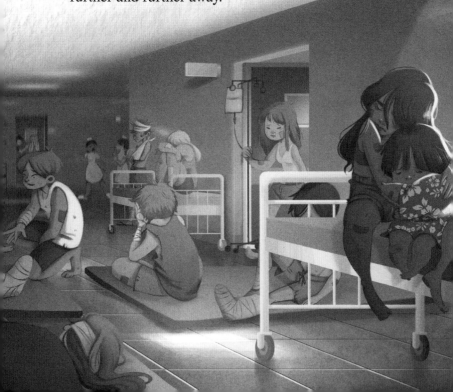

CHAPTER EIGHT

Mom and I were both underwater. I stared in horror at where she was trapped up to her waist in rubble. I pulled at her arms, trying to free her. I was holding my breath, but I was about to run out of air. I had to get her out.

I tugged and yanked at her arms, but Mom wouldn't budge. She pointed upward.

I knew she was telling me to swim up to the surface, but I shook my head. I couldn't leave her.

Mom pushed me away, then pointed upward again.

I shook my head firmly and reached out to grab her arms, determined to pull her free. But just then, a surge of water came at me, like an underwater tsunami. It knocked me away. When I swam back to where Mom was, she wasn't there.

I kept searching. I could feel myself getting light-headed, but I didn't want to stop looking for Mom.

Just a few more seconds, I thought. *Just a moment longer.*

I couldn't give up, but my arms and legs felt heavy. Everything around me was starting to fade. I had run out of time and air.

"Mom," I whispered as my eyes drifted closed.

———————————

I woke up gasping and sweating, sure I would find myself back in the water again. But I was still in my cot.

My mind was still foggy from my nightmare, and it took me a few seconds to remember where

I was and what had happened. *The tsunami. The hospital.*

I glanced around the ward, trying to focus. There were sleeping people everywhere. Each cot held more than one person.

When I turned toward the door, there was a figure walking through it. I gasped. *Mom!*

"Mom? Is that really you?" I leaped out of the cot and ran toward her.

Mom pulled me toward her and wrapped her arms around me. Tears ran down both our cheeks. I squeezed her tightly, trying to reassure myself that she was real.

"Mom!" I cried out. Tears ran down my cheeks. "Where were you? I've been looking for you! I went back to the market but—"

"Yuk and the group of people he was with found me," Mom said. She motioned to Yuk, who stood next to her. "He noticed I fit your description and

overheard me asking about you. When I told him your name and who I was, he brought me here."

I pulled back to study her and realized that Mom was barefoot. One foot was bandaged, and a crutch was tucked under her arm, helping to support her weight.

"What happened to your foot?" I asked.

"It's broken," Mom answered. "When you and I were separated in the water, I was pulled under. I slammed into something—I don't know what. But it was like running into a brick wall."

"How did you get out of the water?" I asked, remembering how hard it had been for me. And I'd been able to use two feet.

"I was determined to find you," Mom said, tearing up again. "I managed to swim to the surface and saw people sitting on the roof of a bus that was floating in the water. They helped pull me onto the roof. We were trapped there for I don't know how long. But eventually a boat came by with two men in it. They rescued us."

I couldn't help but wonder if they were the same men who'd helped Yuk, Noo, and me. Or maybe another team of rescuers. Whoever they were, I owed them a debt of gratitude.

"They took us to a business providing shelter," Mom continued. "That's where Yuk found me."

"Our group had heard that there were injured people waiting for a ride to the hospital," Yuk added. "I was looking to see if Malee was there. . . . but I found your mother instead."

Mom smiled up at Yuk. "I can't thank you enough for helping us. . . . for taking care of my little girl and reuniting us," she said, taking his hand with both of hers. "I hope you find Malee soon."

Hearing her words, my heart plummeted to the pit of my stomach. I had been so relieved to be reunited with my mother that I hadn't realized

Malee wasn't with them. Noo's mother was still missing.

"Thank you. I hope so too," Yuk said. He bit his lip, and his eyes turned glassy. It looked like he was trying to hold back tears. He turned to me. "Thank you for caring for Noo. I need to keep searching, so I am going to another town nearby. My family is there. They can watch Noo while I continue looking for Malee. I must get to the resort."

I hugged him. "Thanks, Yuk," I said. He staggered back, seemingly surprised. "Thank you for everything. My mom and I wouldn't be together now if it weren't for your help. I might not even be here at all."

"I think you would have made it. You would have found a way," Yuk said. "You are a tough girl."

Yuk walked over to the cot and reached out for Noo, picking her up and setting her down next to him. She clutched her father's hand as they walked back over to us.

"Noo, that is Tara's shirt. Please give it back." Yuk pointed to the shirt then to me and spoke in Thai.

Noo started to unbutton the shirt.

"It's okay, Noo," I said, shaking my head. I knelt in front of her and touched her hand. "You keep it." I pointed to the shirt and then to Noo. "It's yours."

Noo smiled. She understood. She motioned for me to come closer, and I leaned in. She hugged me and whispered in my ear, "Thank you . . . Chantara."

CHAPTER NINE

The following morning, I slept late, exhausted from the events of the day before. When I woke up, there was a long line of people in the courtyard outside our ward. Hospital staff members were handing out containers of water.

I shook Mom. "Wake up, Mom! Come on! They're giving out water!"

We scrambled to our feet and stood in line to get a small plastic bottle of water to share between the two us. I was hoping for food too, but there wasn't any. The last time I had eaten was in the market, a full twenty-four hours ago, and my stomach growled angrily. I tried to ignore it as best as I could.

I looked around the courtyard as Mom and I sipped our water. The line was growing longer by the minute. There were definitely not enough people to handle everything.

"Do you think there's anything we can do to help here?" I asked Mom. "Maybe while your foot heals and we figure out how we're getting home? I feel like we should be doing *something*."

"That's a great idea, Tara," Mom agreed. She followed me to the nurse's station, using her crutch to limp along.

The same nurse I'd spoken to when I arrived was still there. She nodded gratefully when I asked if there was anything we could do.

"Many of the nurses, doctors, and hospital staff have not shown up for work," she told us. "They may be injured or searching for their loved ones."

She didn't have to mention the alternative—they could be missing or dead.

Over the next two days, supplies finally began to trickle into the hospital. Mom and I helped distribute water and food to thankful patients.

"If your grandparents were here, they'd be proud to see you helping like this," Mom said.

I held my head high and smiled. "Maybe somehow they know," I said. "I think they'd be proud of you too, Mom."

We talked to other tourists—people from all over the world—as we worked. We helped them write and post flyers for missing family and friends on a bulletin board in the hospital's main lobby. Some of the flyers had photos, and some did not. They all described people who were missing—their names and ages, what they looked like, where they'd last been seen, and how their families and friends could be reached.

Eventually, there were so many flyers that they covered the entire bulletin board and continued onto the walls next to it. And still, the number of flyers kept growing.

Back in our ward, we met a British tourist who'd been staying at the same resort as us. Nolan had been there when the wave hit. The tsunami had destroyed the Thai Orchid, including the bungalows by the pool and beach—the same ones Mom and I had stayed in.

"My family and I were in the bungalows too," Nolan told us. "I wanted to surprise my wife and daughter, Lucy, with breakfast in bed. I woke up early to get food from the resort restaurant while they slept. Before I left, I kissed them both goodbye—gently, so they wouldn't wake up. I was walking back through the pool area when the tsunami hit."

Nolan burst into tears. "It happened so fast. They probably didn't even know what hit them," he wailed. "I didn't know I had kissed them goodbye . . . forever."

Mom placed an arm around Nolan. "I'm so sorry."

I placed my hand on Nolan's. I wished I could take his pain away, but I knew I couldn't. It was a horrible, helpless feeling.

"I hope they managed to get out of the water and are safe somewhere," Nolan said, wiping tears from his face. He pointed at his two broken legs, encased in casts. "I can't even go look for them."

"There are many people out there searching and helping," Mom said, trying to offer some comfort. "Tara and I found one another. They'll find your family too."

That evening, Mom and I said a prayer. We prayed for Malee, Yuk, and Noo, for Nolan and his missing family, for everyone else who had been working and staying at the resort.

Mom lay in the cot next to me. I reached for her hand as I drifted to sleep. "Don't let go," I whispered.

"Never," she replied.

Four days after the tsunami, a nurse in the
hospital finally shared some good news. Flights
were being arranged for foreign tourists. Mom went
to talk with her to get the details.

"An international charity organization is working
with embassies and airlines to provide the flights,"
Mom said when she came back. "It's time for you
and me to go home."

I agreed, but others decided to stay and continue
searching for friends and loved ones. Some wanted
to help find the missing. Others wanted to distribute
supplies to the many people still in need. Those with
medical backgrounds wanted to stay to tend to the
injured.

Later that day, Mom and I rode a bus packed
with other foreigners farther inland to a small,

simple motel in Phuket. We were given our own room with a bed and a private bathroom.

It was heavenly to finally take a shower. We'd been using the hospital bathroom for the past several days, washing in the sink like everyone else. I hadn't had a real shower since the day of the tsunami.

Has it really been only a few days since it happened? I thought as I stood under the warm spray, detangling my hair and washing everything away. *Did I really go through all that?*

I inspected my arms and legs. They were covered in black and blue bruises, but at least the cuts were starting to scab over. Yes, I had survived a tsunami. My injuries—and memories—were proof.

After my shower, I got dressed in the donated clothes and shoes Mom and I had been given. The flip-flops I received were slightly big, but I was just happy to wear fresh, clean clothes and have something on my feet.

Mom had lost her cell phone in the market, so she used the phone at the motel to call Susan, her closest friend back home. Susan knew we were in Thailand, and when Mom finally got ahold of her, I could hear Susan crying through the phone. She had apparently called Mom's cell phone about a million times and had tried to call the resort as well, but couldn't reach anyone there. She was so relieved to hear from us.

Mom arranged for Susan to pick us up from the airport after we arrived and bring us warmer clothing, boots, and coats. The clothes we had been given were good for warm weather, but would not serve us well in the Minnesota winter.

After sleeping on the hard cot at the hospital, the motel bed felt like a puff of marshmallow cloud. Our room had a television, so Mom and I laid down to watch a news report about the tsunami. That was when I realized the full impact of what had happened.

The tsunami had been triggered by an earthquake in the Indian Ocean and had reached fourteen countries. The death toll was unimaginable. In Thailand alone, the number of dead and missing was in the thousands. And they were still counting. The waters had receded, revealing more bodies.

As I watched, I wondered if my dad was watching all of this on the news back home. He didn't even know Mom and I were in Thailand.

I thought too about the Thai people whose homes had been destroyed. Whose lives had been changed or lost. Then I thought about those who had come to Thailand for a vacation, like us. Many were now searching for their family and friends.

One tsunami had resulted in so much death and destruction in so many places. It was difficult to understand.

As we lay there, I realized how easily Mom and I could have been among the missing or dead.

Why were we spared when so many others were not? I wondered.

It wasn't fair. People were suffering, in pain, and yet here I was, showered, clean, and resting on a comfortable bed with my mother. I had the comfort of knowing we were going home soon. Many others would not be.

I couldn't hold in all the emotions bubbling up inside me, all the thoughts swirling in my mind. It all burst out, and I cried.

CHAPTER TEN

Two days later, Mom and I were in a van heading to Phuket International Airport for our flight home. On the way there, it hit me. It was New Year's Day. It didn't feel much like a holiday. Still, we were alive. That was something to celebrate.

"Mom, would it be weird if I wished you happy New Year?" I asked.

Mom placed an arm around my shoulder. "No, honey. Happy New Year to you too," she said. She gazed out of the van window, looking at nothing in particular. We stayed quiet for the rest of the ride.

The airport was just as busy as it had been when we first touched down for our vacation. But this time, the mood was completely different. The tourists I'd seen days ago, filled with excitement and anticipation, were gone. In their place were throngs of people who looked exhausted, dazed, and sad.

Two women huddled close together, their arms around each other. They faced a wall, reading a flyer that asked if anyone had seen the woman and two children pictured on it. As I watched, one of the women wiped tears from her eyes.

We passed by a man pushing a woman in a wheelchair. A bandage was wrapped around the man's arm. The woman had a bandage around her leg. Many others had cuts and bruises on their bodies, like me.

As we waited in line to check in, Mom leaned on her crutch to take the weight off her foot. A boy in line with us had bandages covering both of his hands, including his fingers. The woman with him helped carry his bag since he couldn't use his hands. All of us looked like we had been through a horrific battle and lost.

On our flight to Thailand, Mom and I had each brought a bulging suitcase filled with clothing, shoes, and other necessities. Now we were leaving with one small handheld bag containing the clothing and toiletries that had been donated to us. Not even the bag we carried was ours.

Everyone was quiet as we boarded the plane. There was no chitter-chatter. If anyone did speak, it was a low murmur. When the flight attendant went through the safety instructions, it was dead silent. Even the pilot's voice on the loudspeaker was somber as he made his announcements.

As the airplane taxied across the runway, I thought about Malee, Yuk, and Noo. I wished desperately that we had figured out how to stay in touch. But in the chaos of the hospital, we hadn't thought about it. I hoped Yuk had found Malee . . . that they could have the future they'd dreamed of.

I thought about Nolan and his family and the fishermen who had carried us to safety. Then there were the boy and his grandmother. The shop owner who'd turned his store into a shelter. The people who had helped Mom reach the roof of the bus.

There were so many others who'd banded together to form search parties, who'd volunteered, who'd helped one another in any way they could. I could only hope that they were okay. That they too had found a safe haven somewhere. That they had been reunited with their loved ones.

I stared out the airplane window at the vast ocean below and shivered. Mom and I were so fortunate to be going home. But what about everyone else? What about those who had no home or families to return to?

"Mom, what's going to happen to everyone left behind?" I asked.

"People all over the world are coming together to help with relief efforts," Mom replied. "A lot of countries have offered aid."

"Maybe we can help too when we get home. Like do a fundraiser? Maybe a bake sale. We can figure out how to make the Thai desserts we had at the market and sell them," I said. "It's the least we can do to remember everyone we met. Everyone who helped us. We should never forget them."

Mom gently smoothed away a strand of hair from my face. "We will never forget," she said. "Thailand will recover and rebuild. Thai people are brave, strong, and resilient. Like your grandparents. They're survivors."

"Like us," I said.

"Yes," Mom agreed. "Like us."

A NOTE FROM THE AUTHOR

The 2004 Indian Ocean tsunami was one of world's worst natural disasters. An estimated 230,000 people from fourteen different countries were killed or missing and presumed dead. More than a million were left homeless. Why was the tsunami so devastating to so many countries? No one knew it was coming.

The first—and hardest-hit—country was Indonesia. On December 26, 2004, at 7:59 a.m., a 9.1-magnitude earthquake, one of the largest ever recorded, tore through an undersea fault in the Indian Ocean. The energy was equivalent to 1,500 Hiroshima bombs. It pushed up a gigantic column of water and launched it toward the shore.

Approximately two hours later, Thailand was hit. The waves traveled at speeds of up to 500 miles per hour as they hurtled across the Indian Ocean before slamming into beaches and coastal communities in southern Thailand.

Khao Lak, which is made up of a series of villages on the west coast of Thailand, was the hardest hit. Before the first wave struck, the ocean water receded, exposing the sand. The strange sight caused curious onlookers to venture onto the beach for a closer look. Some collected fish on as much as 1.6 miles of exposed beach. Still others swam in, unaware of the horror that was about to be unleashed.

It is estimated that the sea began retreating at 10 a.m. local time. The ocean water returned in a series of powerful waves less than thirty minutes later. In Khao Lak, some of the waves were as high as 32 feet—about the height of a three-story building.

An estimated 5,400 lives were lost in Thailand. More than 4,000 people were reported missing and nearly 8,500 were injured. The Phang-nga province, where Khao Lak is situated, reportedly lost 25 percent of its residents. Almost 50 fishing villages were severely damaged.

Approximately 2,000 of those who died in Thailand were foreign tourists visting from 37 different countries. The area was especially busy due to the holidays, and many foreigners were staying in low-built bungalows or hotels and resorts close to the water. The location of these buildings, combined with how densely they were built, contributed to the tsunami waves being more devastating in Khao Lak than in other parts of Thailand.

Thailand wasn't the only country impacted. In the eight hours following the earthquake, the tsunami left a trail of death and destruction as far as 5,000 miles from the epicenter. Some of the hardest-hit countries include:

Country	Number of Dead
India	16,389
Indonesia	165,708
Myanmar	71
Maldives	102
Somalia	298
Sri Lanka	35,399

Why was there no warning of the coming catastrophe? Earthquakes cannot be predicted, but tsunamis can be. A warning system was established in the Pacific Ocean in 1948. But the Indian Ocean did not have such a system. Tsunamis were a rare threat in the region. The time between tsunamis in the Indian Ocean has ranged from every few decades to around 500 years.

In 2005, following the deadly tsunami, Thailand created a national disaster warning system. Now, in the event of a tsunami, the public will be warned through the nationwide radio network, television channels, and text messages. Along the coast, warning towers with flashing lights will broadcast announcements in various languages.

Today, Khao Lak continues to recover. Tourists have returned. Hotels, businesses, and roads have been rebuilt . . . with some changes. The once-popular bungalows have been replaced with small hotels raised above the beach and guarded by a defensive wall. Tsunami evacuation routes are marked with signs.

There are reminders of the tsunami, including *Motorboat 813*, a Thai Navy boat that washed up onshore, and the memorial garden surrounding it. There is also a tsunami museum along the main road. The memories still linger and hurt. Nevertheless, the people of Khao Lak continue to move forward and live on, just like Tara and her mother.

Through this story, I wanted to show the power of the human spirit and the good within us, even in the face of the most challenging situations. I also wanted to explore the theme of identity and what ties us to family and our heritage. Tara's story highlights the bond between a mother and daughter as they learn about their Thai heritage and themselves.

As a Filipino-American who was born and raised in the Philippines, I have often wondered what it would be like if I went back. I have not returned since I left as a child. Now I have a son who was born and raised in America. How would he feel if we visited the Philippines? Would we feel awkward and uncomfortable, like Tara? Would we feel like Filipinos or strangers in a foreign land?

The books and articles I read and the images I saw of the tsunami's aftermath as I researched and wrote this story were overwhelming, gut-wrenching, and mind-boggling. There were times when I paused a video or set down a book to give myself a moment to catch my breath, think, and reflect. But I also marveled at the unbelievable survival stories I found. Stories of people who, like Tara, used quick-thinking and determination to survive. People who performed incredible deeds, going above and beyond, to help one another.

I hope this story inspires you to be brave, to do what you can to help others, and to learn more about your own family and their heritage, like Tara did. But above all, I hope it reminds you to pay respect to all those who died, lost someone, or survived the tsunami.

GLOSSARY

bungalow (BUHNG-guh-loh)—a house with a main level and a smaller second level above

debris (duh-BREE)—the scattered pieces of something that has been broken or destroyed

foreign (FOR-uhn)—from another country

fortunate (FAWR-chuh-nit)—having good luck

fragrant (FRAY-gruhnt)—sweet or pleasant in smell

haven (HAY-vuhn)—a safe place

immigrate (IM-uh-grate)—to come from one country to live permanently in another country

luxurious (luhk-SHOOR-ee-uhs)—very fine and comfortable; having an appealing, rich quality

ornate (awr-NEYT)—elaborately or excessively decorated

parched (PARCHD)—very thirsty

refuge (REF-yooj)—a place that provides protection

resilient (ri-ZIL-yuhnt)—able to become strong, healthy, or successful again after something bad happens

rickety (RIK-uh-tee)—in poor condition and likely to break

submerged (suhb-MURJD)—beneath the water's surface

tsunami (tsoo-NAH-mee)—a large, destructive ocean wave caused by an underwater earthquake or volcanic eruption

tuk-tuk (TUK TUK)—in Thailand, a three-wheeled vehicle used as a taxi

ward (WARD)—a large room in a hospital where a number of patients, often needing similar treatment, are cared for

MAKING CONNECTIONS

1. Imagine that a natural disaster were to occur where you live. Write a few paragraphs about what you would do in response. Think about if your community or school has a way to alert everyone. Are there procedures everyone is asked to follow? Are there elements in the emergency response that could be improved? If so, how?

2. Tara had never been to Thailand before and seemed nervous to visit a foreign country. Think about a country you have never visited but would like to. Now imagine you are visiting for the first time. What would you do to learn more about the country, its culture, and its people? What would you like to try or experience?

3. Tara's grandparents were from Thailand. If you returned to where your grandparents, great-grandparents, or ancestors were from, where would that place be? What would you want to learn, discover, or explore there? Who would you want to meet and why?

Cristina Oxtra is the author of the early chapter book *Tae Kwon Do Test,* two biographies for children, *Stephen Hawking: Get to Know the Man Behind the Theory* and *Stan Lee: Get to Know the Comics Creator,* and a Manga graphic novel inspired by Little Red Riding Hood. She is Filipino American and earned her Master of Fine Arts in creative writing for children and young adults from Hamline University. Cristina and her family currently live in the Twin Cities (Minnesota) area.